Dealing with Feelings:

I'm Mad

Written by Elizabeth Crary
Illustrated by Jean Whitney

Dealing with Feelings

Why a book on anger?
Parents often ask me for help dealing with their children's anger. Two factors may contribute to this: (1) Many people were taught to ignore their feelings as children. Now they want to raise their own children differently, but have no idea how. (2) Many people in today's society feel increasingly angry. This includes both parents and children.

How can this book help?
I'm Mad can help children accept their feelings and decide how to respond.

The book models a constructive process for handling anger. It shows a parent and child discussing feelings openly. The story also offers specific options for children. There are verbal, physical, and creative ways described to express feelings. In addition, *I'm Mad* serves as a role model for parents who wish to change the way they respond to their children's feelings.

How to use *I'm Mad*
I'm Mad becomes more useful with time and repetition. A couple of readings probably won't make a dramatic change. But you can start to help your child transfer the information to real life.

Distinguish between feelings and actions. Read the book letting the child choose the options. Ask "How does Katie *feel* now? What will she *do* next?" at the end of each page. More about understanding feelings is below.

Introduce different options. Children need several ways to cope with feelings that work for them. This story offers eleven ideas. When you are done reading, ask your child, "What else could Katie have done?" Record your child's responses on the "Idea Page" at the end of this book.

Use as a springboard for discussing other situations. Begin by discussing something that happened to someone else. Ask your child to identify the feelings and the alternatives the child tried. Talk with your child from the perspective of collecting information, rather than what is right or wrong.

For example, assume a visiting friend, Mike, did not want to go home. Ask, "How did Mike *feel* when it was time to go home?" "What did he do first when he felt upset?" "What else did he do?" Possible answers might be: he ignored the request, he said "No", or he scowled and said "Okay."

When your child can distinguish between feelings and behavior for other people, you can review something he did in the same non-judgmental way.

Elizabeth Crary, Seattle, WA

Katie was excited when she woke up. It was going to be a special day. She hugged her dog Dot and hopped out of bed. Today she was going with her dad to the park. They would have a picnic and play ball and have *lots* of fun.

She was sure the weather would be as wonderful as she felt. It would be sunny and warm. Katie ran to the window to check.

She saw clouds, big black clouds. "Oh no!" she thought. Surely they would go anyway. Clouds wouldn't stop them. She raced over to her dad to find out.

Dad stared glumly out the window. "Dad, Dad, we're going to the park, aren't we?" she asked anxiously. "The clouds won't stop us. You won't let the clouds stop us, will you?"

"Slow down, Katie, and look again," Dad said.

She ran over to the window and peered out again. "Oh, no," she wailed. "Rain! I hate rain!" she yelled. She calmed down for a second and then asked, "We can go anyway, can't we?"

"No," Dad replied. "We can't."

"I'm mad at the rain! And mad at you! Mad, **Mad, MAD!**" Katie yelled.

"You feel mad and disappointed that we can't go to the park. You had the day planned and now you have to make new plans," Dad said.

"I don't have to make new plans. I'll be mad and mean all day," Katie replied.

"It's okay to be mad. You can even be mad all day if you want. What can you do if you don't want to stay mad?" Dad asked.

"I don't know" Katie responded.

What do you think Katie can do?

Listen to any ideas your child has. If he or she has no ideas, turn the page.

"Well, I can think of six things," said Dad. "You could—

Do something physical . . . . page 10

Squish playdough . . . . page 12

Talk about your feelings . . . . page 14

Sing an Un-Mad song . . . . page 16

Ask how other people change feelings . page 18

Plan something fun . . . . page 24

That's a lot of ideas. What will you try first?"

Which do you think Katie will try first?

Turn to the page your child chooses. If no idea is chosen, turn the page.

Do Something Physical

"What is something physical?" Katie asked.

"It's something you do with your body — like stomping your feet or jumping on a trampoline. Many people feel better when they do something physical. Then they don't feel so mad."

"I'm going to stomp my feet," Katie said as she marched around the room saying, "I'm mad! I'm mad! I'm mad!" After marching a bit, she stomped over to Dad and said, "I'm still a little mad. What should I do now?"

"That is up to you, Katie. Do you want some more ideas?" he offered.

"Yes!" she responded.

"You could make up a mad dance or squish playdough," said Dad.

What do you think Katie will do?

Squish playdough . . . . page 12
Make up a mad dance . . . . page 26

Squish Playdough

"I want to squish playdough," Katie announced. "Will you get the playdough for me?"

"Playdough coming up," Dad said as he cleared the table. "See how much of the table you can cover."

Katie plopped the playdough down on the table and began flattening it. "This isn't working," she complained. "I push and push and it is still one big lump. I'm more mad now. Mad at the clouds and mad at the playdough!"

"Would you like a suggestion?" Dad asked.

"Yes!" she answered.

"Divide the playdough into four pieces," Dad explained. "Put one in each corner of the table and then flatten it out. That way you won't have to push the playdough as far."

Katie divided the dough and began squishing it into the corners. When she was done she called, "Dad, come look."

"Hey! You covered most of table," he said. "How do you feel now?"

"Still a little mad," she replied, "I'll do something else."

What do you think Katie will do?

Talk about feelings . . . . page 14
Plan something fun . . . . page 24

Talk About Feelings

"Dot! Dot," Katie called, hunting for her dog. Dot came bounding over to her. She bent over to talk to her. Dot slurped her face with her tongue.

"Dot," she said, pushing her down, "I want to tell you how I feel. I am mad. Mad at the rain. And mad at Dad because he won't take me to the park. What do you think I should do?"

"Woof!" barked Dot, and turned around in a circle.

"You think I should tell Dad how I feel?" she asked. Dot stared at her. "Okay, I'll do it," she said.

Katie ran back to her dad. "Dad, I am mad. Mad at the rain. And mad at you. I'm mad 'cause you won't take me to the park."

"Hmmm," said Dad, "let me get this straight. You want to go to the park, and you're mad because I won't take you."

"Yeah." Then Katie added, "I want to do something fun with *you*."

Turn to page 24.

Sing an Un-Mad Song

"Let's sing an Un-Mad song," Katie suggested.

"Do you know one?" Dad inquired.

"No, I thought you did," Katie answered.

"Uh-oh. I guess we need to make up the words to the song ourselves," Dad said, as he sat down at the piano. "What do you want it to say?"

"Mad, mad feelings, it's time to go away," Katie chanted.

"Okay, how about this?" Dad asked as he began to play *Row, row, row your boat* and sing "Mad, mad, mad fee-lings, it's time to go away!"

"Now say, 'I don't want you anymore,'" Katie added.

Dad finished with, "I've had enough today." Then he suggested, "Let's sing it all together."

Mad, mad, mad feelings, it's time to go away.
I don't want you anymore. I've had enough today.

"It worked! I'm not mad, but I'd still like to make up a Mad Dance. Can we, Dad?" Katie asked.

"Sure we can," Dad smiled.

Turn to page 26.

Ask for Help

"Dad, when I'm mad, what can I do to get un-mad?"

"Well," Dad replied slowly, "that deserves some thought. Maybe you need to collect ideas from more people. Mrs. Bennet is next door and Aunt Lora is probably home too. You can ask either of them."

Katie thought a moment and then called her aunt on the phone. "Aunt Lora, I am mad. I wanted to go to the park with Dad today, but it's raining. I need ideas on how to get un-mad."

"I can tell you what works for me," Aunt Lora replied. "When I'm mad at home, I take a nice, warm bubble bath. The warm water feels so good, it washes the unhappy feelings away. When I am not at home, I imagine the mad feelings drifting away from me."

"How do you do that?" Katie asked.

"Well, It's like blowing your mad feelings into a balloon, tying it off, and then letting go and watching it blow away."

"Thanks, Aunt Lora. That sounds fun." Katie hung up.

What do you think Katie will do?

Wash away the mad feelings . . . . page 20
Let the feelings go . . . . page 22

Wash Away the Mad Feelings

Katie wanted to take a warm bath.

"Dad, is it okay to take a bath now?" she asked.

"Sure," he responded. "Do you want me to start the bath water?"

"Yes," she answered and ran off to find the bubble bath.

She hopped into the tub. The bubbles reached her chin. She could feel the warm water wash away the mad feelings.

After she got dressed, she went to see her dad. He asked, "How's my girl? Still feeling mad?"

"No. It really worked. I don't feel mad now. I want to do something special with you though. Could we?" she asked.

"Sure. What would you like to do?"

Turn to page 28 and find out.

Let the Mad Feelings Go

Katie found a balloon. She blew into the balloon, but nothing happened. She tried again. Nothing happened. She tried harder and harder, but still nothing happened. "This isn't fair," she thought. "I was trying to get rid of my mad feelings and now I am *more* mad. Let me see, what can I do? I can quit or I can ask for help."

Katie decided to ask her dad to start the balloon. "Dad, I want to blow my mad feelings into the balloon, but I can't get it started. Will you do it?"

"Happily," Dad replied. He started the balloon and passed it to Katie. When Katie finished blowing the balloon, Dad tied it off. "Now what?" Dad asked.

"I'll show you. Come with me," she invited. Katie took the balloon outside. She walked down to the garbage can. She lifted the lid and said, "I am going to dump the mad feelings in here." After she put the balloon in, she put the lid back on. "Now the mad feelings are all gone."

"That was pretty clever. Do you have any ideas about what you want to do today?" Dad asked.

Turn to page 28 for Katie's answer.

Plan Something Fun

"What can we do?" Dad mused. "Something fun *and* something to help your mad feelings go away. If I were a magician, what would you ask for?"

"A magic spell to make the mad feelings disappear!" Katie replied excitedly.

"Let me see," Dad said, as he picked up a book and pretended to look for an answer. "Is that a talking spell or a doing spell?"

"Both," Katie giggled.

"The book says the best spells are singing an 'Un-Mad' Song or dancing a Mad Dance. Either will do the trick," Dad said.

"But Dad," Katie answered, "I don't know an Un-Mad Song or a Mad Dance."

"That is a solvable problem. Which do you want to start with?" Dad asked.

What do you think Katie will do?
Sing an Un-Mad Song . . . . page 16
Dance a Mad Dance . . . . page 26

Dance a Mad Dance

"How do you do a Mad Dance, Dad?" Katie asked.

"I don't know. Let's make up one," Dad answered. He went to the stereo and put on a tape with marching music. "How should we start?"

"With lots of stomping, to get the mad out. And then some twirling," Katie decided.

"Okay, stomping and twirling. Is this a dance where we do the same thing or different things?"

"Same thing. You follow me. If I make a mad face, you make one too," Katie directed. "Then we will trade."

Katie marched around the room stomping and pounding her hands. Dad followed right behind. Finally she stopped stomping and said, "Your turn to lead now."

Dad alternated stomping and twirling. He twirled more and more. When the music was over, Katie was so dizzy, she fell to the floor giggling.

"That was fun," she laughed. "I could never be mad after a dance like that. I want to do something else fun."

Turn to page 28.

Have a Pretend Picnic

"Dad, can we have a pretend picnic?"

"Certainly," he replied.

"Maybe even a real *inside* picnic," Katie added.

"Sure, pumpkin. We have the food. All we need to do is fix it and pack it into the picnic basket," Dad said.

"Let's pack it right now," Katie suggested.

Dad and Katie made the sandwiches, peeled carrots, and mixed lemonade. Then they packed the food, paper plates, and everything else in the basket.

When the lunch was made, Katie said, "I will draw some pictures to make a park." When she was done, Katie hung the pictures on the wall.

At lunch time they took the basket and discussed where the best view would be. They chose to sit facing the lake picture.

Katie turned to her dad and said, "This is as much fun as a picnic in the park. I'm not mad anymore. I really just wanted to be with you."

The End

Idea Page

Katie's ideas:

- Yell and stay mad
- Stomp her feet
- Squish playdough
- Talk about her feelings
- Sing an Un-mad song
- Ask for help
- Wash away the mad feelings
- Blow feelings into a balloon
- Do something fun
- Dance a Mad Dance
- Have a pretend picnic

Your ideas:

-
-
-
-
-
-
-
-
-
-
-
-
-
-

Feelings and the Parent's Role

One of your jobs is to help children understand and deal with their feelings. Children need basic information about feelings, they need to have their feelings validated and they need to have tools to deal with those feelings.

Develop a vocabulary. Children may feel overwhelmed or scared by feelings. One simple way to begin understanding feelings is to label them.

- Share your feelings: "I feel frustrated when I spill coffee on the floor."
- Read books that discuss feelings—for example, the *Let's Talk About Feelings* series.
- Observe another's feelings: "I'll bet he's proud of that A+ grade."

In addition, introduce your child to different words for related feelings—for example, mad, furious, angry, upset, etc.

Distinguish between feelings and actions. Understand that feelings are neither good nor bad. Feeling mad is neither good nor bad. However, hitting is a behavior. Hitting is not acceptable. You can say, "It's okay to be mad, but I cannot let you hit your sister."

Validate the child's feelings. Many people have been trained to ignore or suppress their feelings. Girls are often taught that being mad is unfeminine or not nice. Boys are taught not to cry. You can validate children's feelings by listening to them and reflecting the feeling. Listen without judging. Remain separate. Remember, your child's feelings belong to her/him.

When you reflect the feeling ("You are mad that Stephanie has to go home now"), you are not attempting to solve the problem. Reflecting, or acknowledging the feeling helps the child deal with it.

Offer children several ways to cope with their feelings. If telling children to "Use your words" worked for most kids, grownups would have little trouble with children's anger. Children need a variety of ways to respond——auditory, physical, visual, creative, and self-nurturing. Once a child has experienced a variety of responses, you can ask him or her what she would like to try.

For example: "Do you want to feel mad right now or do you want to change your feeling?" If your child wants to change, you could say, "What could you do? Let's see, you could run around the block, make a card to send to Stephanie, talk about the feeling, or read your favorite book." After you've generated ideas, let the child choose what works for her. Often all children need is to have their feelings acknowledged.

Be gentle with yourself. Remember, some situations are resolved quickly and others take time and repetition. Hold a vision of what you would like for your child and yourself, and acknowledge the progress you have made.

Coping with intense feelings ...

Dealing with Feelings books acknowledge six intense feelings. Children discover safe and creative ways to express them. Each interactive story allows the reader to choose the main character's actions and see what happens as a result. Useful with 3–9 years. 32 pages, illustrated. $6.95 each. Written by Elizabeth Crary.

ISBN 0-943990-62-9, paper

ISBN 0-943990-64-5, paper

ISBN 0-943990-66-1, paper

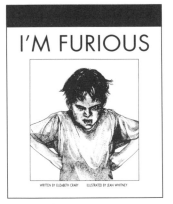

ISBN 0-943990-93-9, paper

ISBN 0-943990-89-0, paper

ISBN 0-943990-91-2, paper

Library-bound editions available. Call Parenting Press, Inc. for information.

Ask for these books at your favorite bookstore, or call 1-800-992-6657.

VISA and MasterCard accepted with phone orders. Complete book catalog available on request.

Parenting Press, Inc., Dept. 201, P.O. Box 75267, Seattle, WA 98125.

In Canada, call **Raincoast Books Distribution Co.,** 1-800-663-5714.

Prices subject to change without notice.